Dear Reader:

Welcome back. As you may remember, the money paid to buy the first two Super Spy books has been put toward the cost of adopting a child.

I'm excited to say that my wife and I will have some big news to share with you by the time the third book is finished.

I offer you my humblest thanks for reading *Santa Claus: Super Spy: The Case of the Delaware Dinosaur* and for helping us start a family of our own.

Enjoy the story.

Sincerely,

Ryan Jacobson

www.operationadoption.com

Super Spy Secret Code

1 = A	10 = J	19 = S
2 = B	11 = K	20 = T
3 = C	12 = L	21 = U
4 = D	13 = M	22 = V
5 = E	14 = N	23 = W
6 = F	15 = O	24 = X
7 = G	16 = P	25 = Y
8 = H	17 = Q	26 = Z
9 = I	18 = R	

Can you solve this secret message from Santa Claus?

The first letter is filled in for you.

B
2-5   2-18-1-22-5   23-8-5-14

,

25-15-21–18-5   19-3-1-18-5-4 .

Santa Claus:
SUPER SPY

The Case of the
Delaware Dinosaur

by Ryan Jacobson
Illustrated by Erica Belkholm

LAKE 7 CREATIVE
Mora, Minnesota

For Lora:
my love, my life.

ISBN 0-9774122-1-0

1 2 3 4 5 6 10 09 08 07 06 05

Printed in the United States of America, Worzalla, Stevens Point, WI.

July 2006

Super Notes from Super Readers

"I really liked your book. I think my dog did too."

Callie, Age 10

"The best thing about the book is that it has a lot of excitement in it. When I feel happy, the book makes me feel even better."

Emily, Age 9

"Your book was so good I couldn't stop reading it!"

Lauryn, Age 8

"After reading the first chapter I wanted to read more. I read your whole book. I really liked the story."

Sam, Age 9

*Ryan would love to hear from you! You can write to him on the Internet at **www.santaclaussuperspy.com**.*

Santa Claus: Super Spy

Santa has a secret. He's a Super Spy. With the help of boys and girls across the country, he protects the world from danger.

Now, armed with Super Spy watches and gadget belts, Santa and his top agents Paul Jenkins and Emily Swanson must save the state of Delaware from a terrible danger.

Contents

Santa Claus: SUPER SPY

1
Time to See the Dentist

Emily Swanson was scared.

Yes, she was a top-secret Super Spy. Yes, she had met Santa Claus, Ervin the Elf, and Santa's reindeer Comet. And yes, she did help her new friend Paul Jenkins save Florida from Jack Frost and the Florida Freeze.

But that didn't mean Emily liked going to the dentist. Just thinking about it scared her even more.

Now she didn't want to leave the house. She'd be happy to sit in the tiny, yellow kitchen all day. She'd even wash the dishes.

"Mom, can I please stay home? I don't want to go," Emily cried.

Her mother Jayne was a beautiful, 29-year-old kindergarten teacher. Jayne's long, blonde hair was a perfect match to Emily's.

Emily dreamed of becoming like her mother. She even wanted to teach some day. But right now Emily was upset.

"It'll be good for your teeth," said her mother Jayne. "There's nothing to be afraid of."

That's not what Emily thought. The girls in her older sister's reading club, the Book Worms, had told Emily all kinds of horror stories about dentists.

Of course the Book Worms were making up the stories. But Emily didn't know that. She believed all dentists were evil!

"Please Mom," begged Emily, "I feel sick. Can we do it another day?"

Jayne replied, "You're scared. That's why you feel sick. And you need to take care of your teeth. So we're going today."

"No," Emily yelled, "I'm not!"

That did it. Jayne was mad.

"Emily Swanson, you are seven years old! Start acting like it. Or maybe you'll find yourself on Santa Claus's naughty list next Christmas."

Santa, thought Emily, *he could get me out of this. If only my watch would beep. If only it were time for my next mission.*

But Emily's watch didn't beep.

Her mom opened the door and said, "Let's go."

3

2
Something's Coming

It was a busy day in Wilmington, the largest city in Delaware.

Stores and restaurants lined the streets. Cars of all sizes and colors filled the roads. Hurrying men and women crowded the sidewalks. Some were shopping. Others were on their way to work.

The state of Delaware was located on the east coast of the United States. It was famous for its beautiful beaches and state parks.

Delaware was the second-smallest state in the country. But plenty of wild animals lived there.

Many of them had strange and funny names like horseshoe crabs, muskrats, egrets, and blue hen chickens.

But today Delaware was about to become famous for another kind of creature.

*****

"Run for your lives," the man shouted as he ran into a nearby street.

A teenage boy driving a black pickup slammed on his brakes. He nearly crashed into the scared man. But the man kept running, weaving his way between cars and other trucks.

The man yelled, "It's coming!"

"What is that crazy fool doing?" asked a crabby, old lady standing outside a shoe store.

No one else could blame her for asking. The

man was acting oddly. And it wasn't every day that they saw a chubby man, wearing a suit and tie, running down the road.

Some people began laughing at the man.

Then, all of a sudden, the street began to rumble.

Thump!

Thump!

Thump!

The sound grew louder, as it came closer and closer.

Then all was quiet, until...

The people stopped laughing.

They all started to run.

3
Case #2

Emily was almost to her mom's minivan.
She usually enjoyed taking trips with her mother.
She could sit in the back and watch her favorite
movies. Or she could talk to her mom about school
and horses and what she wanted for her birthday.

But today Emily was not excited to climb
inside. She was dreading it.

Then it happened. Her watch began to beep.

She almost shrieked with glee. It was time for
her next case! Her trip to the dentist would have to
wait.

As Emily thought about her next adventure, she became more and more eager to go. She missed her friend Paul. She couldn't wait to see him again.

But now she needed an excuse to get away from her mother.

"Mom," Emily said, "I forgot my stuffed bear Teddy. Can I go inside to get him?"

Her mother answered, "Okay but come right back."

Emily didn't reply. She knew that she would not be coming right back.

She ran into the house and checked her Super Spy watch. She wrote down all of the numbers that Ervin the Elf had sent her.

9-14 20-8-5

2-1-3-11 25-1-18-4

Next, she pulled the Super Spy Secret Code out of her pocket. She remembered, *A is 1. B is 2.*

C is 3, and so on. That means the first letter is I. The second is N. So the first word is "in."

Emily kept at it until she had decoded the whole message, I-N T-H-E B-A-C-K Y-A-R-D.

In the back yard, Emily thought, *Ervin must be waiting for me there.*

She hurried out the back door, and there he was. The little elf was no more than three feet tall, dressed all in red and green. His sharp nose and pointy eyes made him look as if he were getting into trouble.

Comet was there too. The famous reindeer stood proudly in front of Santa's magic sleigh. He looked larger than Emily remembered. But that could've been because he was standing next to an elf.

Emily was amazed that the neighbors couldn't see her strange visitors. Then she thought about what Santa had told her on their last mission. No people could see Ervin or Comet, as long as they were near the invisible sleigh. It was part of the sleigh's magic.

But several dogs and cats gave Ervin and Comet very odd looks. Animals could see through the magic.

And of course Emily was wearing her Super Spy watch. So she could see through the magic too. Ervin and Comet appeared to her as plain as day.

"Hi Ervin," smiled Emily. She was glad to see her little friend.

"Hello and hi, Emily Super Spy," sang the elf. "Your next case is here. Let's get in gear."

Emily's heart leapt with excitement. She hopped into the sleigh, and off they went.

12

4
Together Again

Within minutes Emily, Ervin, and Comet arrived at the North Pole. Comet led the sleigh into a tiny opening in the snow. The opening seemed much too small, yet somehow the sleigh managed to fit through it.

Emily was once again inside Santa's wonderland. It was like paradise: toys and dolls over here, chocolate and candy over there. Everything a child could want was in that room.

Then she spotted Paul. He was tall for an eight-year-old boy and very handsome. Emily loved how brave he was. She also thought his dark, curly hair was cute. Emily didn't like very many boys. But Paul was one of her best friends.

She gave him a quick hug.

"Paul, why are you here?" asked Emily. "I thought we were going to pick you up."

"Santa asked me to come," the boy answered. "He had to tell me a secret."

"Really? What secret?" asked Emily.

"I'll tell you later," Paul replied. Then he added, "Santa also said you and I are his best spies. That's why we're getting another case."

"Santa said that?" Emily asked. But she wasn't surprised. After all, the two of them had solved *The Case of the Florida Freeze*.

"Yes," Paul told her. "And he promised to show us an invention."

Santa Claus peeked into the room. Emily thought she would never get used to seeing him. His long, white beard curled just above his belly button. His chubby cheeks looked like two tomatoes. His shirt was white, and his pants were red.

Santa's face beamed with joy.

"Welcome back Emily," hollered the jolly, old man. Then he added, "Both of you, please come this way."

The duo skipped behind Santa. They followed him into a large, white room. It was empty inside, except for three heaping piles of toys and one very large machine.

The machine looked like a giant freeze ray. It was 10 feet tall, and the top was shaped like a pop bottle that was being poured onto the floor. Buttons and gizmos dotted the entire machine.

"Have you ever wondered how I get all of the presents into my sleigh?" he asked them.

"Not really," said Paul.

"Me neither," answered Emily.

Santa continued, "I'm going to show you."

He walked to the machine.

"This is called the Shrink Wrapper," said Santa. "We blast toys with a ray from this machine. It shrinks them to the size of a quarter."

He added, "Then we push the 'wrap' button. It covers the toys with wrapping paper. Of course we don't do that for every gift. Not all children get their presents wrapped."

Santa took a tiny, orange box out of his pocket. It was smaller than a spider.

"See? This one has already been Shrink-Wrapped."

Both children shared the same thought. *I wonder if that present is for me!*

But it didn't matter. Paul and Emily agreed that Santa's invention was the best machine ever.

"How do the presents get big again?" asked Emily.

Santa grinned. "That's a secret for another time. Right now, we'd better get to work."

With that, the three of them entered the Super Spy Secret Base.

5
The Mission

Santa's secret base looked nothing like the rest of his workshop. There were no toys or candy anywhere.

The first thing the children saw was a large map of the world. It was hanging on the back wall. Tiny lights flashed all around it.

Dozens of computers lined each of the room's side walls. Above them were shelves stacked to the ceiling with books. It looked as if Santa had more books than a library.

"What do you two know about dinosaurs?"

asked the jolly, old man.

Paul loved dinosaurs. So he was the first to answer. "They look like giant lizards. Some of them eat meat, like the *Tyrannosaurus rex* or *T. rex* for short. He's the meanest one of all."

"Good," said Santa, "what else?"

Emily spoke next. "They're extinct. That means they aren't alive any more."

"Right," Santa told them, "at least that's what I thought. A monster was seen in the state of Delaware. It might be a dinosaur."

"A dinosaur?" Paul asked with excitement. "That's cool."

"No, it is not cool," Santa replied. "If we're up against a dinosaur, this case will be dangerous."

Emily chuckled and said to herself, *A dinosaur can't be any scarier than a dentist.*

Santa pressed a button on a nearby computer.

The map of the world became a map of Delaware.

He asked Emily, "What can you tell us about the state of Delaware?"

"We talked about Delaware in school," she

replied. "It was the second state ever to become part of the United States. Dover is the capital."

"Very good," said Santa. "Everything the two of you know will come in handy on this case."

Emily wondered aloud, "Is the dinosaur in Delaware a meat eater?"

"We're not sure," Santa told her. "In fact, that's part of our mission. First we'll find out what kind of dinosaur it is. Then it's up to us to catch it."

6

A Dinosaur!

Santa Claus, Paul, and Emily put on their jackets. Then they buckled their gadget belts around their waists.

Each of the green belts was lined with 12 square pouches. Inside each pouch was a different gadget. The Super Spies could use the gadgets if they got into trouble.

Paul and Emily had used some of the gadgets before. For instance, Shoe Flies helped them fly. And Trouble Bubble bubble gum made a gummy, sticky mess. It was good for trapping villains.

23

"Remember what I told you about the gadgets," said Santa.

Paul replied, "We remember. We shouldn't use them unless we have to. Or they'll run out of energy."

"That's right," said Santa. "Each gadget lasts only a short time. You wouldn't want to use it without good reason. You might need it later."

Soon the Super Spies were ready. They climbed into the magic sleigh.

With two quick gallops Comet leapt into the air, pulling the sleigh behind him.

Santa steered his reindeer south, and they were on their way to Delaware.

"Santa," Emily asked, "is this mission really going to be dangerous?"

"Yes it is," answered Santa. "But don't worry. If we work together as a team, we'll be fine."

Within minutes they arrived. Wilmington was directly below them.

Emily spotted the wide Delaware River. It flowed toward the Atlantic Ocean.

She also saw colorful houses everywhere. Cars filled the busy streets. And tall buildings reached toward the sky.

Then Emily let out a gasp. A monster was standing in the middle of town!

It was giant, green, and taller than many of the houses. It had short arms and a very large head. Its mouth was filled with razor-sharp teeth.

It was a *Tyrannosaurus rex*. And it was destroying everything in sight.

The huge beast looked at Santa's magic sleigh. And it let out a roar!

Emily heard Santa say, "Oh dear."

7

Is Everyone Safe?

Santa Claus sped his sleigh past the dinosaur and farther into the city.

He noticed an empty stretch of road several blocks from the *T. rex*. So he guided his sleigh to the ground. It quietly skidded to a stop.

Emily was the first to climb out. She saw stores, factories, and hotels all around her.

Dozens of cars were parked in the street. But none of them were moving. The cars were empty, and there were no people nearby. In fact, there didn't seem to be any people anywhere.

The vacant area made Emily feel alone. Her knees started to shake.

"Where is everyone?" she whimpered.

"Hopefully they've gone far away from here," answered Santa. "But we'd better make sure. We'll sneak toward the dinosaur and take a closer look."

"How are we going to stop that thing?" Paul asked.

"I don't know yet," admitted Santa. "But first things first. We must see to it that the people are safe. Ervin and Comet will wait here, in case we need backup."

"Do you think I should wait with them?" Emily asked nervously.

"No, they'll be fine," replied Santa. "You can come with us."

That was not the answer Emily had wanted to hear.

Santa and the Super Spies crept toward the fierce beast.

"Remember," Santa told them, "if you get into trouble use your Trouble Bubble bubble gum. Blow the biggest bubble you can."

Emily replied, "I don't think it will do much good against a dinosaur."

"You're probably right," said Santa. "But at least Ervin and Comet will know that you need their help."

Soon the trio was just two blocks from the dinosaur. They couldn't see it behind all of the buildings. But they could hear it growling and roaring.

The Super Spies rounded a corner. And they were almost trampled by a crowd of scared people.

None of the people gave the Super Spies a glance, as they ran away from the *T. rex*.

"They're so scared that they didn't even see us," said Paul.

"It's a good thing," noted Santa. "It would be hard to explain what we're doing here, without giving away that we're Super Spies."

"I don't blame them for running," added Emily. "I don't want to get eaten by the dinosaur either."

Santa, Paul, and Emily checked the rest of the area. No one else was around. It looked as if everyone had gotten away.

Suddenly Emily realized that the dinosaur had become very quiet. The growling and the roaring had stopped.

Then she saw a shadow creeping toward them. Her heart skipped a beat. The shadow looked big and mean and scary. It was shaped like an animal with a long mouth and sharp teeth.

Before she could warn the others, the shape leapt at her. It landed only a few feet away.

Emily screamed. She was face to face with the creature. But it wasn't the dinosaur. It was a dog, and it didn't look friendly.

8
Rex the Dog

The dog was half Emily's size. Its messy, golden fur shined in the sun, and its pointy ears were a tangled mess.

The dog glared at the Super Spies and growled.

"He's not very nice at all," said Emily.

"I wouldn't say that," replied Santa. "I'm sure he's a very good dog. But he's scared. And being scared makes some animals act mean."

"Look at his collar," noted Paul. "It says his name is Rex."

32

Paul was right. The dog was wearing a collar. Printed on it were the letters R-E-X.

"If he has a collar and a name, then he must be someone's pet," added Emily. "Maybe we should help him get home."

Santa answered, "Your heart is in the right place Emily. But it's best to leave Rex alone. After all, you don't know if he'll bite you."

Santa was right, but Emily still wanted to help the dog. She wanted to give him a hug. She wanted to tell him that she was scared too.

Instead she looked kindly into his eyes, and she tried to smile.

Slowly Rex's expression changed. He stopped growling, and he tilted his head sideways. He let out a soft whimper and started wagging his tail.

His eyes softened. Rex looked at Emily as if he wanted to be her friend.

The dog took two steps toward the young Super Spy. Emily reached out to pet him. But Rex stopped in his tracks.

His eyes hardened, and they darted away from Emily's gaze. He looked left then right. And he ran away, back the way he came.

"Oh, no," cried Emily, "I thought we were going to—"

The Super Spies looked up. Staring down at them was the giant *T. rex*. Its mouth opened wide. And another loud, piercing sound filled the air.

"Run for it!" yelled Santa.

And they ran.

Santa Claus:
SUPER SPY

9
The Hungry Beast

The *T. rex* snarled and bit down. Santa jumped back, barely avoiding the dinosaur's sharp teeth.

Emily started to cry as the Super Spies ran. The dinosaur followed. It was hungry.

"What are we going to do?" screamed Emily.

"I don't know," said Santa. "Just keep running!"

They couldn't stop, not even for a second. The dinosaur was right behind them. But all of a sudden, Paul turned to face the beast.

"I'm not afraid of that thing," he shouted.

He took his Trouble Bubble bubble gum out of his gadget belt. Then he popped the gum into his mouth.

The dinosaur stopped, surprised by Paul's actions. The beast stared at the boy, waiting for him to make his move.

"Paul, no!" yelled Santa.

But Paul didn't listen. He started blowing the biggest bubble he could. He blew, and he blew, and he blew.

Emily watched as Paul's bubble grew in size. First it was a baseball then a basketball. Soon Emily was looking at a Trouble Bubble bigger than a car.

Please let this work, wished Emily. *Let the dinosaur get stuck in Paul's Trouble Bubble.*

The bubble was about to explode, when the dinosaur decided to act. It lifted its huge left foot and stepped on the Trouble Bubble, squashing it. With a loud POP, the entire bubble disappeared under the *T. rex's* sharp, clawed toes.

"It... It... It... didn't work," Paul muttered.

"I know," yelled Santa. "Now run!"

Santa, Paul, and Emily hurried away. But the Trouble Bubble didn't even slow the *T. rex* down.

The great beast lifted its foot, ripping away from the gummy, sticky mess. The monster continued its chase of the Super Spies.

The trio passed building after building, running as fast as they could.

Emily was tired. She wanted to peek behind her. But she was afraid of what she might see. The dinosaur could be right next to her, about to take a bite. So she kept running.

At last they spotted an open door. It led into an old, broken-down factory.

"Quickly," said Santa, "into that doorway."

They charged inside.

The building was dark and empty, except for dust and spider webs. The air was thick with the smell of mold.

But at least the doorway was too small for the dinosaur. They were safe.

Or so they thought.

BOOM!

BOOM!

BOOM!

The building began to shake.

"What's going on?" cried Emily.

"It's the dinosaur," said Santa. "He's hitting himself against the building. He's going to knock it down on top of us!"

10
A New Gadget

There wasn't much time. Soon the old factory would crumble and fall.

"We have to make a plan," said Santa Claus.

"What kind of plan?" asked Emily.

"We need to find a way out of here," he answered.

The roof began to crack. Each time the dinosaur hit the building, the crack grew larger. Pebbles from the ceiling rained onto the Super Spies. Then a chunk of roof crashed to the floor, almost landing on Santa.

41

"I think we'd better hurry," added the not-so-jolly, old man.

"Maybe we can use one of our gadgets," said Emily.

"Right," replied Paul, "how about our Shoe Flies? We can fly out of here with them."

Emily answered, "I don't like that idea. Flying will only get us closer to the dinosaur's mouth."

"Let's try a gadget we haven't used before," suggested Santa. "Each of you, take out your You-You."

"Is that like a yo-yo?" asked Paul.

"Yes, sort of," answered Santa. He pulled a tiny, round object out of his gadget belt. It looked very much like a red yo-yo, except a camera lens was sticking out of it.

Santa continued, "When you roll this gadget, it makes another you, a fake you, a You-You."

"Is it like a hologram?" asked Paul.

"Yes," replied Santa, "it's a picture of you that moves."

"How does it work?" asked Emily.

"The camera lens snaps a photo of the person who rolls it. Then it makes a movie of that person, which it projects into the air. The You-You rolls back and forth. And the hologram moves with it."

"Oh, I see," said Emily. "We'll roll our You-Yous out the door. The dinosaur will think they are us, and it will chase them. Then we can sneak back to the sleigh."

Santa nodded.

"That sounds like a good plan," agreed Paul.

"But what will happen to Us-Us? I mean our You-Yous?" asked Emily.

Santa told her, "Just like a yo-yo goes back and forth, so does a You-You. Our You-Yous will go out the door a little ways. Then they'll roll back here. They'll roll out again. Then they'll come back."

"How long with that last?" wondered Emily.

"The You-Yous will keep going until they run out of energy. Then the holograms will disappear," replied Santa.

"Let's try it," said Paul.

The three Super Spies rolled their You-Yous out the door.

11
Back to Safety

Holograms of Santa, Paul, and Emily appeared above the You-Yous. The young Super Spies couldn't believe it. The holograms looked just like them.

The *T. rex* was surprised too. Its eyes widened, and it chased the You-Yous.

The beast snapped its jaws at the holograms. But it couldn't find anything to bite.

"Let's go," whispered Santa.

The trio tiptoed away from the scene. They reached the next street, and they ran toward the sleigh.

Emily peeked behind her, and she almost started to laugh. The *T. rex* was jumping back and forth, trying to eat the holograms. But it couldn't catch them. The dinosaur looked very confused.

Soon Santa and the children were back at the sleigh. Ervin was waiting for them, and he was holding a piece of paper.

"The dinosaur attacked. But you all made it back," sang Ervin. "I've got some good news, that I must share with you."

"What is it Ervin?" asked Santa.

"The computer on the sleigh, I used it today," the elf told him. "A dinosaur doctor I found. She lives right in town."

"A dinosaur doctor?" asked Santa. "Do you mean a paleontologist, someone who studies old dinosaur bones?"

"That's what I mean. You are very keen."

47

Ervin handed Santa the piece of paper. It was a computer printout. Santa studied it for a moment. Then he smiled.

"A job well done Ervin. The doctor's name is Jen Nissen. I know her well."

"You do?" asked Emily.

"Yes," Santa answered, "many years ago she was a Super Spy too."

"Wow," both children said in surprise. They'd never met a grown-up Super Spy, besides Santa.

"Ervin, I think you and Paul should pay Doctor Nissen a visit," Santa told the elf. "Maybe she knows where the *T. rex* came from. And maybe she knows how to stop it."

"Should I go too?" Emily asked hopefully.

"No, you can stay here with me."

Emily almost started to cry. She wanted to go away with the others. Anywhere but here.

She was about to say so. But Santa added, "I need your help. We have to keep the dinosaur busy, so it won't cause any more trouble."

Emily did not like the sound of that.

12
The Dinosaur Doctor

In the blink of an eye, Paul and Ervin arrived at the Howard Institute, the place where Doctor Nissen worked. The building was large and made of dark, red bricks.

Paul and Ervin jumped out of the sleigh. They hurried across the beautiful, green yard. And they dashed into the building.

The two of them wandered the halls, looking for Doctor Nissen's office. What they saw amazed them. Fossils were put together to look like life-sized dinosaur skeletons. And hundreds of dinosaur drawings covered the walls. Paul decided that the Howard Institute must be a dinosaur museum.

Soon Paul and Ervin found the office. Paul knocked on the door. He heard the soft, gentle voice of Doctor Nissen say, "Come in."

The doctor didn't look at all the way Paul had expected. She was about 40 years old. She was tall and skinny with long, dark hair tied behind her head. Paul thought she must be the prettiest woman in the world.

Doctor Nissen was not surprised to see them. She gave her visitors a warm smile.

"An elf and a young boy? You must be a Super Spy," Doctor Nissen said to Paul. She flashed her old watch at him.

"Yes I am. And we need your help."

"I suppose you're here about the *Tyrannosaurus rex*," added Doctor Nissen.

"How do you know about that?" asked Paul.

The doctor laughed. "It's been on all the news channels. Besides, the dinosaur came from here."

*****

"I don't know if I can help you," Emily admitted to Santa Claus. "I'm scared."

Santa grinned. "I have just the thing. I grabbed these out of the sleigh before the others left."

He held up a new pair of pants. They were shiny, blue, and covered with sparkles. The pants were beautiful. And they were just Emily's size.

Santa added, "These are called Fraidy Pants. If you put them on, you won't be afraid any more."

"Are they magic?" asked Emily.

"Not exactly," answered Santa, "but they are for you."

"Can I try them on?" she asked excitedly.

"Certainly," he told her, "there's a bathroom in that building over there. Go inside and change. I'll wait here."

Emily felt better already. She grabbed the pants from Santa. And she ran into the building across the street.

13
How to Stop a Dinosaur

Paul was shocked by what he had heard. "The dinosaur came from here?" he asked Doctor Nissen.

"Yes," the doctor answered, "it did."

She shared her story with Ervin and Paul. "About 15 years ago I started my job at the Howard Institute. I came to work one day, and I found a dinosaur egg in front of my office. Needless to say I was surprised. I didn't know any better. So I took it into my office, and I put it in a warm, safe spot."

"Where was that?" asked Paul.

"I wrapped the egg in a blanket. Then I hid it

inside my desk. I didn't think anything would come of it. But one day the egg started to shake. A few minutes later it cracked open. Out popped a baby *T. rex*. It was a real dinosaur!"

"That would be exciting," Paul added.

The doctor continued, "The *T. rex* became a pet to me. I loved it in the same way that some people love dogs. I fed it. I played with it. I cuddled it to sleep. But I had to keep my dinosaur a secret."

"Why?" Paul asked her.

"If anyone else found out, they'd take it away from me. They'd want to study it," she answered. "I let the little *T. rex* stay inside my office. But that became harder as the dinosaur grew. By the time it was six months old, the *T. rex* needed a bigger place to live."

"What did you do then?" asked Paul.

"My family owns a large warehouse a few

miles from here. I moved the *T. rex* into there. The warehouse was bigger than a school gym, and the dinosaur had more than enough room to run and play. It seemed very happy."

"Didn't the dinosaur want to eat you?"

Doctor Nissen replied, "Oh, I had to be quite careful. I kept the dinosaur well fed, so it was never hungry. But within two years it was bigger than I am. That's when I began keeping a safe distance away from it."

"Good idea," noted Paul.

"After that everything was fine, until a year ago. The dinosaur started growing too quickly. It became as large as a house. I knew I couldn't keep it any more."

"Were you going to give it away?" Paul asked.

"I wasn't sure what to do. Then yesterday, when I went to feed it, my dinosaur was gone!

Someone had opened the large warehouse doors, and the T. rex escaped. I've been trying to think of a way to catch it ever since."

"Did you come up with a plan?" asked Paul.

"I think so," said Doctor Nissen. "I've been working all day on a giant sleeping pill. If you can get the T. rex to swallow it, the pill should put the dinosaur to sleep."

"That won't be hard," said Paul. "The monster will eat anything."

"Don't be too sure," replied Doctor Nissen. "Dinosaurs don't like medicine any more than boys and girls do."

Paul laughed. "We'll find a way to get the T. rex to eat that sleeping pill."

"Of course you will," answered Doctor Nissen. "You're a Super Spy."

14
Dead End

Emily was proud of her sparkly, new Fraidy Pants. They were just her size.

Excited to show them off, she ran out the building and into the street. She still felt a little afraid. But she didn't want to tell Santa that his gadget wasn't working.

Emily reached the other side of the street. Then she realized there was a problem. Santa Claus wasn't there.

Where did he go? Emily said to herself. But her thoughts were interrupted. She noticed that she was standing in a very large and very scary shadow. She heard a loud, terrible noise.

Emily spun around. Standing behind her was the dinosaur. The beast was less than 50 feet away. It almost seemed to smile as it licked its lips, hungry for a meal. Then it charged.

Emily didn't have time to scream. She turned and ran. She scanned the nearby buildings looking for an open door, anywhere to escape.

She was afraid to look behind her. But she could hear the heavy thumps of the dinosaur's feet. They were getting closer.

Emily turned left into an alley between two tall buildings. It grew dark as the sun became hidden from her view. Garbage covered the dirty walkway. The air smelled like rotten eggs.

But there was even more trouble for Emily. Ten feet ahead of her, a big brick wall blocked the alley. She had run into a dead end.

"Oh, no," she cried.

Emily turned to go back the way she had come. But it was too late. At the front of the alley, the dinosaur was waiting. It slowly stalked toward her. Its jaws snapped open and shut.

Emily was about to become the dinosaur's dinner. She let out a scream!

Then something moved in the corner to her right. She hadn't seen it before, but Emily was not alone.

The dinosaur closed in, and out jumped Emily's rescuer. It was Rex the Dog.

The brave hound landed between Emily and the dinosaur. Rex growled his fiercest growl.

The dinosaur kept coming.

15
Rex vs. T. Rex

Emily was trapped in the alley with Rex the Dog. They were about to become dinosaur food.

Her mind raced with thoughts of her family, Santa Claus, and Paul. She was scared, not only for herself but for Rex too.

If anything happens to me, Emily thought, *I hope Rex will be safe.*

The monster was only a few steps away. It opened its mouth to bite Emily. She closed her eyes.

All of a sudden Rex let out a loud bark. Emily opened her eyes and saw him jump toward the dinosaur. He dodged the beast's gaping mouth. He rolled under its belly. And he sunk his teeth into the dinosaur's left toe.

The *T. rex* howled in pain. It jumped back, forgetting about Emily. It turned to face the dog.

Rex scooted between the *T. rex's* legs and under its large, thick tail. He darted out the alley.

The dinosaur roared again. It backed its way out from between the buildings. Then it turned and chased the dog down the empty street.

Emily was safe. But she worried about Rex the very brave dog. He had saved her. But now the dinosaur was going to eat him!

She had to do something, so she started to run after them.

I'm not scared, Emily realized. *The Fraidy Pants must be working.*

From behind her, something tapped her

shoulder. She turned, expecting danger. Instead she was happy to see that it was Santa Claus.

"Emily thank goodness you're all right," he said, huffing and puffing. "I hid when the dinosaur came back. I saw it chase you away from the building. And I've been trying to find you ever since."

"I'm fine Santa," Emily answered. "Rex the Dog saved me. But now he needs our help."

Before Emily could explain, the magic sleigh flashed before their eyes. It skidded to a stop in front of them.

Paul and Ervin hopped out of the sleigh. "Santa, Emily," Paul shouted, "we know how to stop the dinosaur."

16
Santa's Plan

The four quickly exchanged stories. They had to act fast to save Rex the Dog.

"We must get the dinosaur to swallow the sleeping pill," said Santa Claus.

"But dinosaurs don't like medicine," added Paul. "That's what Doctor Nissen told us."

"Don't worry. I have an idea," Santa answered. "I'll fly the sleigh around the dinosaur's head. It will try to bite me."

"That sounds dangerous," noted Emily.

"It's no more dangerous than what Paul and

you must do. Use the Shoe Flies from your gadget belts, so both of you can fly. Together you'll carry the giant sleeping pill to the dinosaur's mouth. When it tries to bite me, you can throw the pill down its throat."

Santa gave the children a moment to think about the plan. Then he asked Emily, "Do you think you can do it?"

"I can do anything Santa," she answered. "I'm wearing my Fraidy Pants."

Santa smiled as he hopped into the sleigh. "Put on your Shoe Flies. Grab the sleeping pill. And follow me."

Emily and Paul took the Shoe Fly stickers out of their belts. The little stickers looked like bird wings. The Super Spies stuck them onto their shoes.

They each lifted an end of the sleeping pill. The large, white pill was lighter than Emily expected. It was an oval shape and almost as big as Santa. But it weighed less than a bag of groceries.

"Are you ready?" Paul asked.

"Yes," she replied.

The duo jumped into the air. They suddenly felt the wind beneath them. And a cool, wet breeze tickled their faces. They were flying.

The Super Spies stayed behind Santa, as he steered Comet toward the dinosaur.

Within seconds, they spotted the great beast and their new friend Rex. He was running in circles, dodging the dinosaur's bites. The *T. rex* snapped its jaws at Rex, barely missing the brave dog.

Emily could see that Rex was getting tired. "Santa hurry!" she yelled.

The sleigh darted toward the *T. rex* and began looping around its head.

The dinosaur ignored Santa.

Then the sleigh bumped into the beast's head, scraping just above its left eye. The *T. rex* roared! It turned its gaze toward Santa Claus.

Rex saw his chance to escape. He wagged his tail at Emily. Then he bolted toward the nearby buildings. Rex disappeared between them.

17
Trouble for Santa

Santa Claus continued his dangerous flight around the dinosaur's head. The *T. rex* snapped and snarled. It almost caught Santa with its teeth. The creature opened its wide mouth.

"Now," yelled Santa.

Paul and Emily sped toward the gaping mouth. They flung the sleeping pill inside before the monster could shut its jaws.

The beast crashed its teeth together. Its eyes

widened as it tasted the foul medicine. But the dinosaur didn't swallow. It spit the pill onto the street below. Their plan hadn't worked.

Once again the dinosaur turned toward Santa. The old man wasn't ready for the beast's next attack. The *T. rex* caught the sleigh in its mouth.

Comet was able to break free. But Santa was trapped.

The dinosaur shook its catch back and forth. Santa slipped out of the sleigh and nearly fell to the ground. He grabbed an edge, and he held on for dear life.

Paul and Emily flew toward their leader. But Santa waved them away. It was too dangerous.

The dinosaur shook the sleigh again, trying to knock Santa loose. It wasn't after the metal sleigh. The *T. rex* wanted meat.

Santa was losing his grip. Emily knew that she

had to do something. As fast as she could, she flew to Ervin the Elf.

"Do you have any spare gadgets?" she asked.

"They're in the sleigh, up that way," he answered, pointing toward Santa.

Emily leapt into the air. She sped toward the dinosaur's mouth, where Santa hung helplessly.

"I told you to stay away!" he shouted.

"I will," answered Emily. "Throw me a You-You."

"A You-You?" asked Santa.

"There's no time to explain. Just do it!"

The old man reached into the sleigh. He opened a secret box under his seat.

The dinosaur gave another shake, and Santa almost fell again.

He reached into the box. He pulled a You-You into his hand. And he flung it toward Emily.

75

"Thanks Santa," she yelled. And she darted to the slobbery pill below.

The dinosaur gave the sleigh one last shake, and Santa slipped. He dropped toward the ground.

As if in slow motion, Santa saw the beast throw the sleigh. Then the dinosaur reached toward him with its large, powerful jaws. Santa was about to become dino dinner!

Suddenly Paul swooped in with his Shoe Flies. He caught Santa in midair.

"I've got you," he said as he dove away from the beast.

The dinosaur had been robbed of its dinner. It roared in anger.

"Hey dinosaur," Emily's voice boomed, "down here!"

The creature spotted the young Super Spy. She was running back and forth on top of the pill.

In a blur of movement, the *T. rex* lunged toward Emily. She didn't have time to get away. The monster's wide open mouth scooped up everything in sight.

Emily and the pill vanished inside the beast's jaws. The dinosaur had swallowed them whole.

18
The Sleeping Dinosaur

Santa and Paul both cried out for Emily, but it was too late. She was gone.

The dinosaur began to stumble. It lazily swayed left and right. Its eyes rolled back in its head.

The *T. rex* fell face-first onto the street, crashing to the ground with a loud THUMP!

Doctor Nissen's sleeping pill had worked. The dinosaur was asleep. But that didn't matter to Santa and Paul. Their friend Emily had been eaten by the *T. rex*.

They both began to sob, until they heard a

familiar voice behind them. It said, "Wow, that was close."

Santa and Paul quickly turned around. They were amazed to see Emily smiling at them.

She was alive!

They ran to her and gave her the biggest hug of her life.

"What happened?" asked Paul. "We saw the dinosaur eat you!"

"No, you saw the dinosaur eat Me-Me... I mean a You-You of me. I rolled the gadget onto the sleeping pill, so the *T. rex* would think I was there."

Santa laughed. "Ho! Ho! Ho! That was quite a good trick Emily and very brave of you. You saved the day."

Emily smiled brightly, and she seemed to stand a little taller too.

But their troubles weren't over yet.

"What will we do with the *T. rex* now?" asked Paul. "It's going to wake up soon."

"That's a good point," said Santa. "I don't have any ideas. Do you?"

"Can't we just bring it back to the dinosaur doctor?" Emily wondered.

"No," answered Paul. "Doctor Nissen couldn't take care of it any more. The *T. rex* was too big."

"Too big?" asked Emily. That gave her an idea. "What if the *T. rex* were smaller?"

Santa chuckled. "I know what you're thinking Emily, and I like it."

The three Super Spies came up with a plan. They checked Santa's magic sleigh for damage. It was chewed up, and there were plenty of dents and scratches. But the red and gold sleigh still looked good enough to fly.

Santa Claus tied Comet to the front of the sleigh. He clued Ervin in on their idea. Then, in the blink of an eye, Ervin and Comet were once again on their way to the North Pole.

19
A "Small" Problem

Within minutes Ervin and Comet had made it to the North Pole.

And soon they were back in Wilmington, where Santa and the children waited.

The elf landed the sleigh next to the sleeping monster. Emily noticed that something very important was missing.

"Did you bring the Shrink Wrapper machine?" Emily asked Ervin.

"The ray was too big. It wouldn't fit in our rig," he responded.

"Now what are we going to do?" wondered Paul. "Without the Shrink Wrapper, our plan won't work."

"I did bring the ray," Ervin chimed, "in a different way."

He held out his tiny elf hand, showing them a very small Shrink Wrapper.

Santa laughed his hearty laugh. "Ervin you used the Shrink Wrapper to shrink itself."

"That is correct. I hope it's not wrecked."

Santa replied, "I'm sure it's fine Ervin."

"The Shrink Wrapper can shrink itself?" Paul asked.

"Of course it can. Do you remember using your Reflector mirror against Jack Frost?"

"Well, it was a robot of Jack Frost. But I remember," noted Paul.

Santa grinned. "The Reflector works for a

Shrink Wrapper too. Ervin blasted the Reflector. And the ray reflected back to make the Shrink Wrapper smaller."

"Wow," said Emily, "that was good thinking Ervin."

The elf bowed, as if to say, "You're welcome."

"Will the Shrink Wrapper work if it's this little?" Emily asked Santa.

"No I don't think it will," he told her. "It's time to show you another of my secrets."

Santa dug into his gadget belt. He pulled out a tiny, red squirt bottle.

"What's that?" asked Paul.

"This little gadget is called a Growth Squirt," said Santa. "When a present is Shrink-Wrapped, I can squirt it with this. The present will return to normal size."

"Cool," said Paul, "do you think we can have

one of those too?"

"I'm afraid not," Santa answered. "This is the only one I've ever made."

At that moment, the dinosaur began to stir.

"We'd better get moving," said Santa. "Stand back."

He squirted the Shrink Wrapper. With a shake and a rattle, the machine grew before Paul and Emily's eyes.

It was a strange sight to behold. The machine didn't grow all at once. Instead, bits and pieces grew at different times. For instance, the top grew faster than the bottom. And the machine almost tipped over.

But within a few seconds the Shrink Wrapper was back to its original size.

"Hurry," yelled Paul. "The *T. rex* is getting up."

The sleepy dinosaur was on its feet, shaking

its head back and forth. It still wasn't quite awake. But if the Super Spies didn't act fast, there would be more trouble very soon.

Santa Claus dashed behind the Shrink Wrapper. He aimed it at the beast, and he fired.

With a bright flash of white light, the *T. rex* seemed to vanish.

But after the smoke cleared, Emily spotted the dinosaur. The little creature was less than two inches tall. Its ferocious roar sounded more like a cat's meow.

Santa walked to the dinosaur and picked it up with his hand. Emily and Paul followed him to get a closer look.

"Oh," said Emily, "isn't it cute?"

20
Back Home

"It looks like this case is closed," said Santa.

"Yes," answered Emily, "but what are we going to do with the *T. rex*?"

"I think Doctor Nissen will want the dinosaur back since it's so small," he told the young Super Spy. "I'll return it to her. But first we'd better get Paul and you home. After all, you still have a dentist trip to take."

"I know," Emily agreed. "And with these Fraidy Pants I'm not afraid any more."

Santa blushed. "About those paints..."

"You don't need them back, do you?" she asked.

"No, it's nothing like that," he replied. "You see, your Fraidy Pants aren't really Fraidy Pants. They're ordinary pants with sparkles. In truth, there's no such thing as Fraidy Pants."

"You mean these pants didn't make me brave?" she asked.

Santa smiled. "No, you did that all by yourself."

"How can you say that?" she cried. "I wanted to run away and hide."

"Everyone gets scared. Even I do," Santa answered. "But when we are scared, we do our best anyway. That's what makes us brave, and that's what makes us Super Spies."

Santa Claus was right. Emily had been scared. But she still helped catch the Delaware Dinosaur. She was brave after all.

"I guess it's time to go," said Emily.

"I suppose it is," Santa answered. "But before you leave, someone wants to say goodbye."

He pointed toward the buildings in the distance.

Emily turned and saw Rex the Dog bounding toward her, his tail wagging with excitement. She kneeled down and opened her arms. Rex jumped into them.

She hugged the dog that had saved her life.

Santa scratched Rex behind his ears. "Don't worry," he told Emily. "I'll make sure that Rex gets home safely. And I have a feeling you'll see him again soon."

Emily let go of Rex. "I'll miss you," she told him. "You're a good dog."

Rex licked Emily's face one last time. Then the Super Spy stood up. She held out her wrist while Santa wound her watch backwards.

"I'm rewinding your Super Spy watch to the moment you left your house," he told her. "You'll go back in time to that instant. It will seem like you were never gone."

Almost at once, Emily started to fade away as the watch brought her home.

Suddenly she remembered. "Stop! Paul you were going to tell me about the—"

It was too late. Emily was in her house again. She'd have to wait for their next adventure to learn about Santa and Paul's secret.

Right now it was time to visit the dentist. Emily walked outside and to her mom's minivan. She climbed in.

"That was quick," her mother told her. "Where's your stuffed bear?"

"I decided I don't need Teddy," Emily said. "I can do this on my own."

Her mom smiled warmly. "Good for you, Honey. By the way, I like your pants."

"Really?" asked Emily. "They're nothing special."

Emily's mother backed the minivan down the driveway. The two of them began their trip to see the dentist.

EPILOGUE

"I was wondering if you'd stop by," Doctor Nissen said as Santa Claus walked through her office door.

The jolly, old man answered, "It's good to see you Jennifer. I'm here to return your dinosaur."

He handed Doctor Nissen the tiny *T. rex*. And he added, "Do take better care of it this time."

"I will," she promised.

Santa Claus turned to leave. But he stopped.

He looked back at the doctor and said, "Paul told me the dinosaur's story. There are a couple of details that trouble me. I'm hoping you can help."

"I'll do my best," answered Doctor Nissen.

"The egg, you said that you found it outside your office door," Santa noted.

"That's right," she replied.

"Do you have any idea where it came from? Before you found it, I mean."

Doctor Nissen told him, "I'm afraid I don't."

"And what about the warehouse doors? Do you know who let the dinosaur out?"

"Again," replied the doctor, "I can't help you."

Santa frowned. "That's too bad."

"What about you?" Doctor Nissen asked. "Do you know who might have done it?"

Santa didn't respond. Instead he smiled one last time and said, "I suppose that's a case for another day. Thank you Jennifer."

Santa bowed. Then he vanished out the door.

Coming Soon!

The Case of the
Colorado Cowboy

Visit our website to learn about
the next exciting adventure,
coming soon!

www.santaclaussuperspy.com

Dynamite Dino Facts

1. *Tyrannosaurus rex* means "tyrant lizard king."

2. *T. rex* lived about 65 million years ago in a time called the Cretaceous period.

3. These predators grew to be about 40 feet long and 20 feet tall (the size of a small house).

4. *T. rex* had small arms that were only about three feet long. Their hands were made up of two long fingers and one very short finger.

5. *T. rex* was a carnivore (meat eater). It ate other dinosaurs, using its large teeth and sharp claws.

6. The first *T. rex* fossils (bones) were found in the United States more than 100 years ago.

7. *T. rex* fossils have been found in the United States and Canada.

Super Spy State Challenge

Test your Super Spy knowledge with these questions about the state of Delaware. If you get stumped, you can find the answers using the page numbers provided.

1. What is the capital of Delaware? (Page 22)

2. What ocean borders Delaware? (Page 25)

3. What is the largest city in Delaware? (Page 4)

4. What river flows through Wilmington? (Page 25)

5. True or false? Delaware is the smallest state in the United States. (Page 4)

6. True or false? Delaware was the second state ever to become part of the United States. (Page 22)

7. Delaware is located on the _____ coast of the United States. (Page 4)

8. Name two animals commonly found in Delaware. (Page 5)

Got 'em all? Check your answers at the website **www.lake7creative.com/answers**.

Visit the Super Spy Website:
www.santaclaussuperspy.com

Check out all of the fun activities you can do when you visit Kids' Corner at the *Santa Claus: Super Spy* website:

- Join the Super Spy Fan Club.
- Solve more Super Spy codes.
- Read what people are saying about the books.
- Take the Kids' Poll and send your book ideas.
- Write author Ryan Jacobson a message.
- Create your own Super Spy adventure.

Be sure to get your parents' permission
before you visit the site.

Bonus Drawing

In the first version of this book, Paul and Ervin rescued Emily and Rex from the alley (Chapter 15). But the author Ryan later decided that he wanted Rex to be the hero. (He loves dogs.) So he changed that part of the story.

About the Author

Ryan Jacobson loves to write. He would write all day and all night if he could! In fact, Ryan has been writing stories since he was 16 years old.

Ryan says, "If you want to be a good writer, you should read books and write as often as you can."

Ryan lives in Mora, Minnesota, with his wife Lora and their dog Boo.

ATTENTION EDUCATORS:

Schedule a guest appearance by author Ryan Jacobson at your school, book fair, or special event.

Ryan is an experienced presenter who will lead a fun, interactive, and informative discussion about the process of writing and creating a book.

For more information, visit the Lake 7 Creative website at **www.lake7creative.com/school**.